GOD'S
WILDEST
WONDERMENT
OF ALL

GOD'S WILDEST WONDERMENT OF ALL

PAUL THIGPEN

ILLUSTRATED BY
JOHN FOLLEY

TAN·BOOKS

Illustrations by John Folley.

Graphic design by Caroline Green.

ISBN: 978-1-5051-1470-6

Published in the United States by
TAN Books
P. O. Box 410487
Charlotte, NC 28241
www.TANBooks.com
Printed and bound in the United States of America

I praise You,
for I am wonderfully made.
– Psalm 139:14 –

For my children, grandchildren,
and godchildren: Lydia, Elijah,
Michael, Francisco, Sofia, Santiago,
Lucia, Avila, Brian, Elizabeth,
Phillip, Isabel, Derek, Kiel,
Reginald, and Dominic.
– Paul Thigpen –

For my sister, Cat, who loves
God's creatures deeply,
and for my wife, Deirdre.
– John Folley –

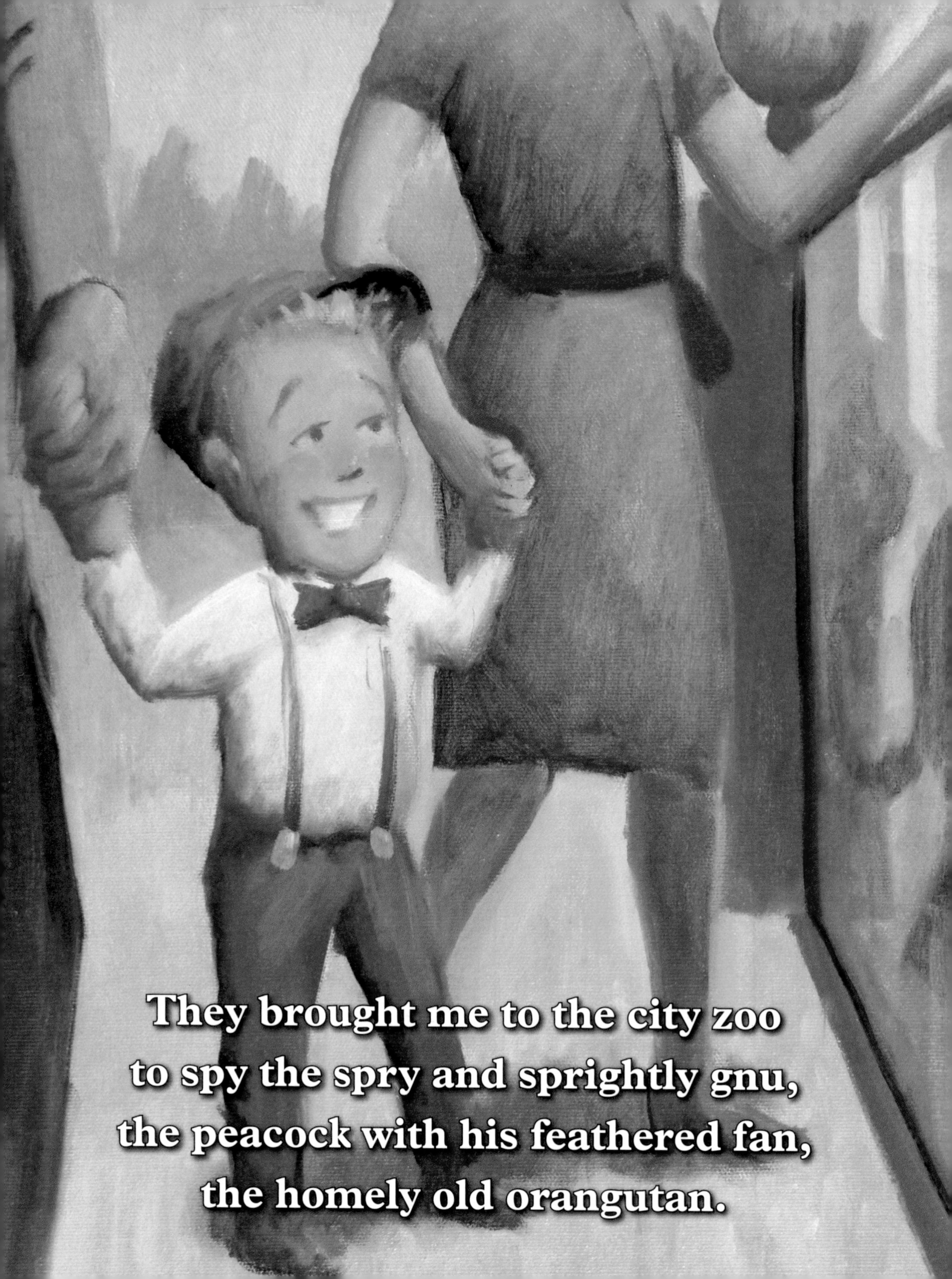

They brought me to the city zoo
to spy the spry and sprightly gnu,
the peacock with his feathered fan,
the homely old orangutan.

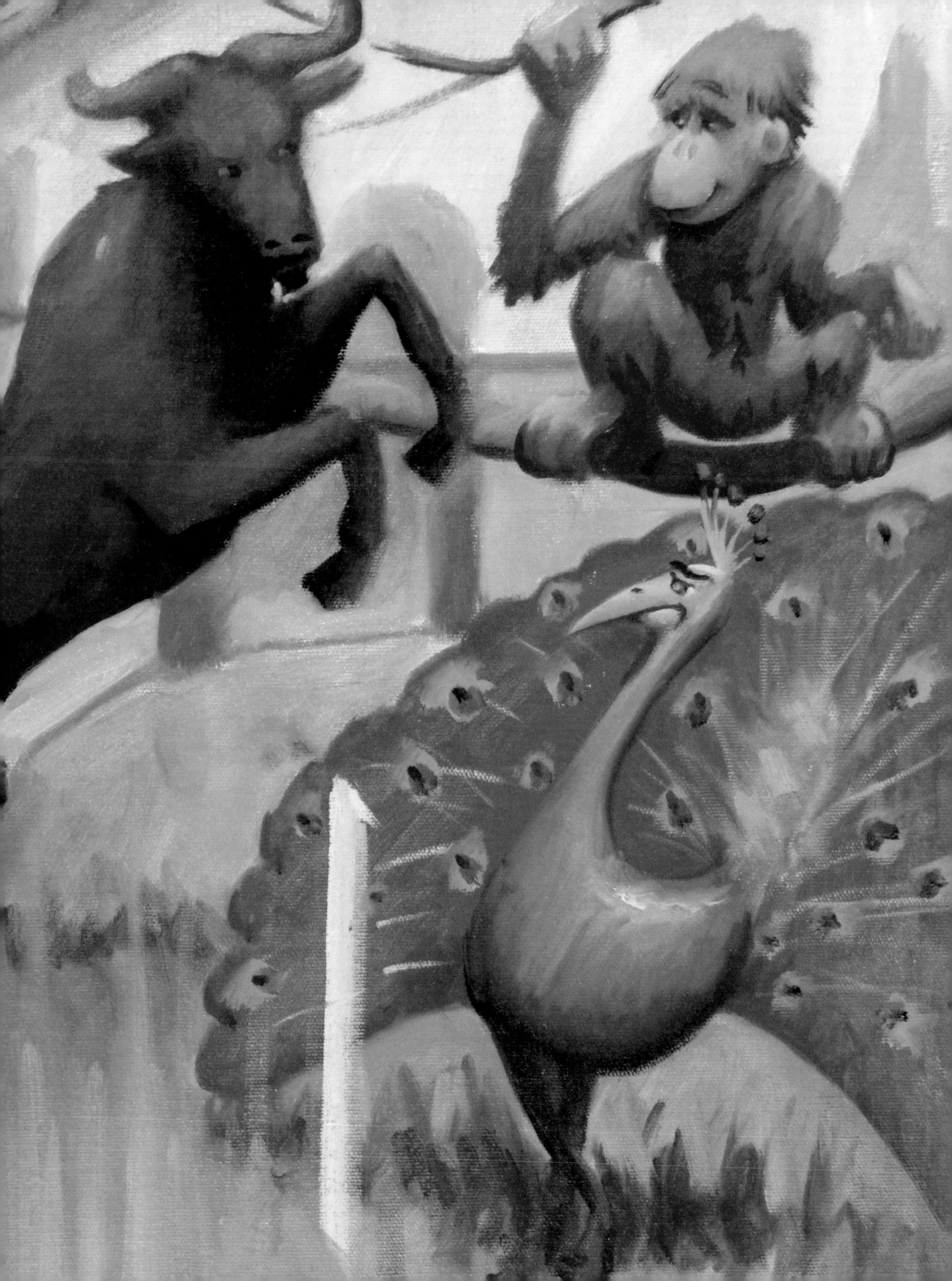

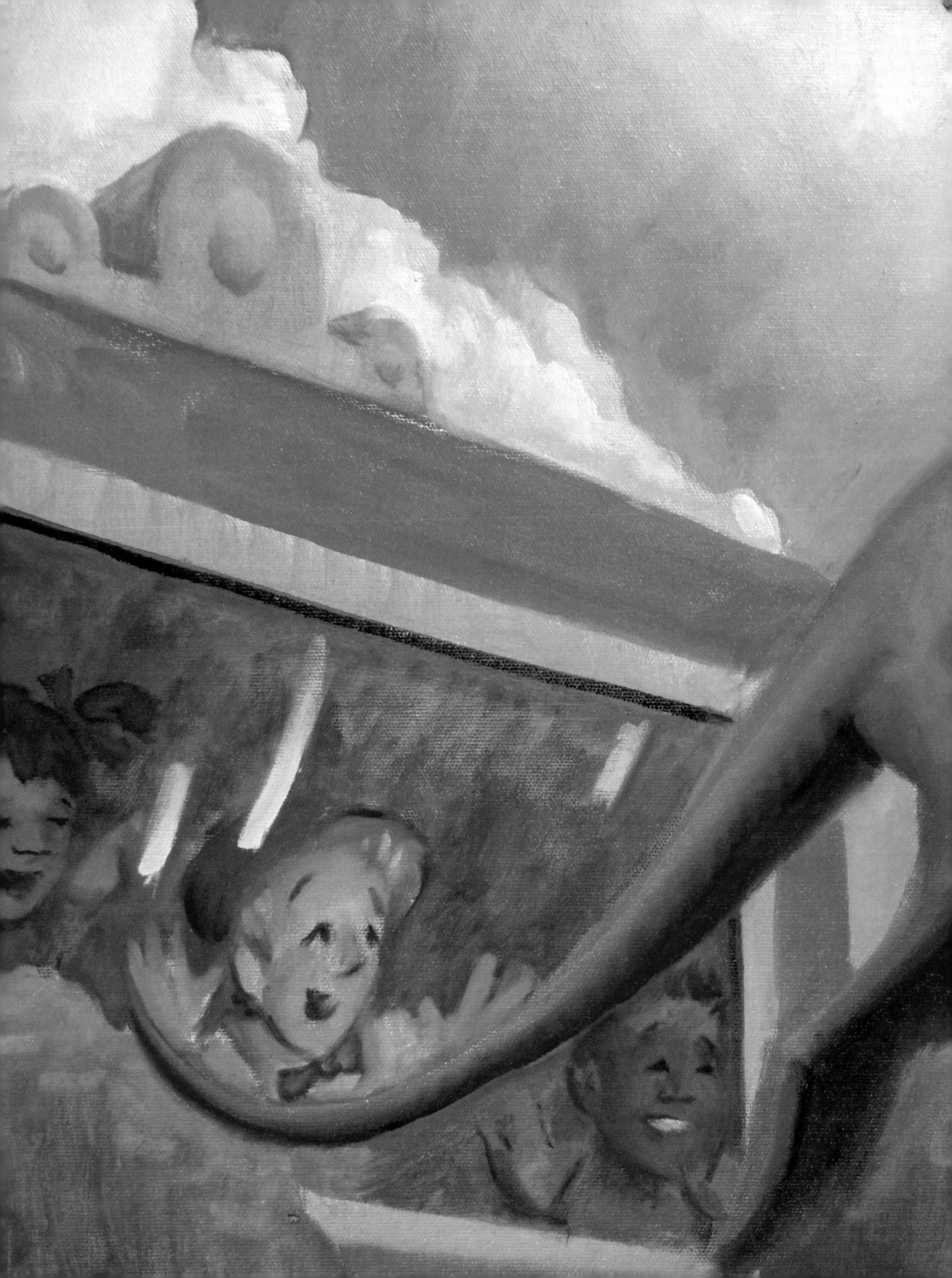

But while I smile at bird and beast
I cannot fathom in the least
the reasons why the Lord would choose
to bless the world with kangaroos.

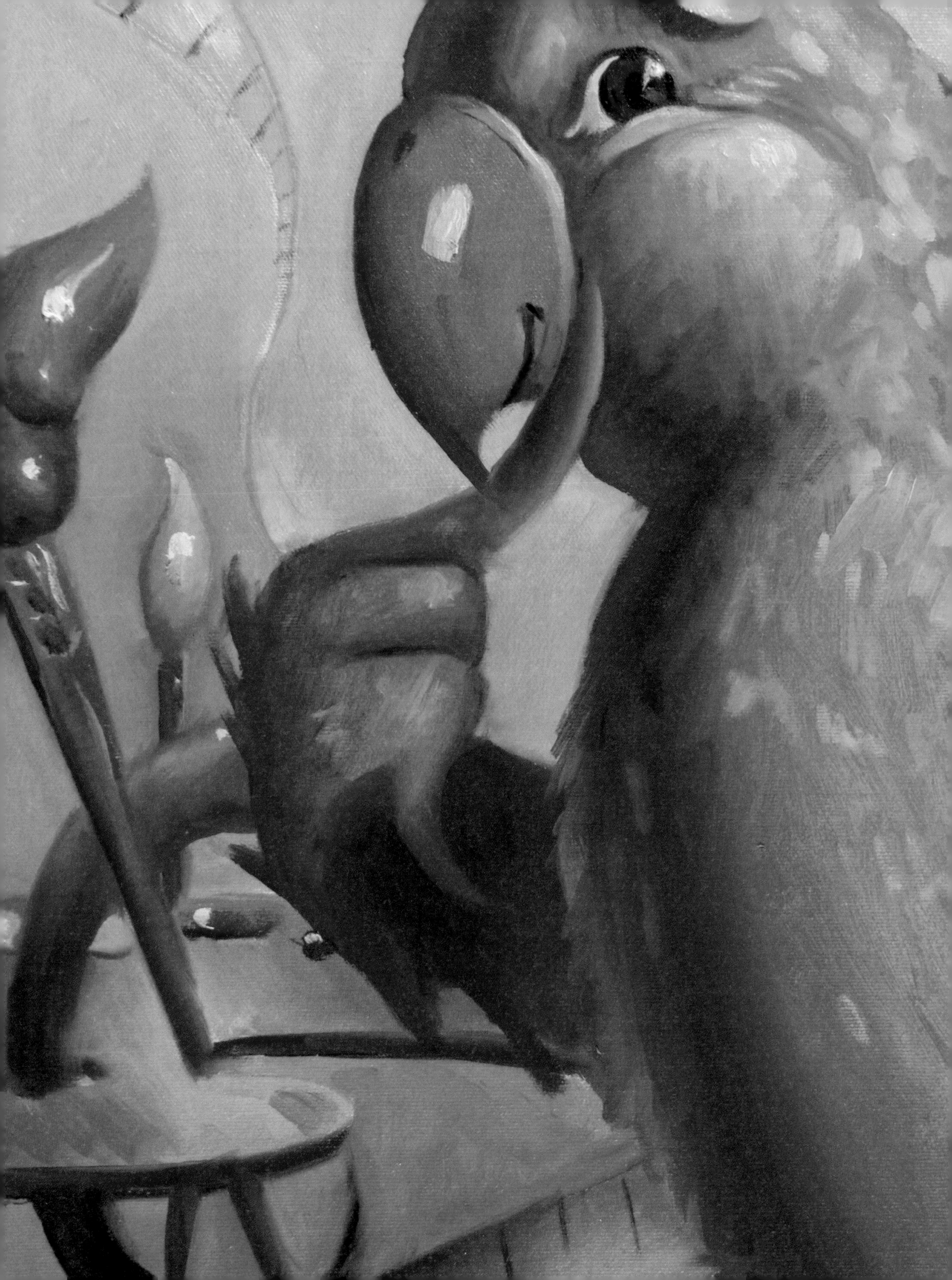

How odd of God to spend His time
in painting parrots gold and lime
or fitting snakes inside a skin
that soon will come right off again!

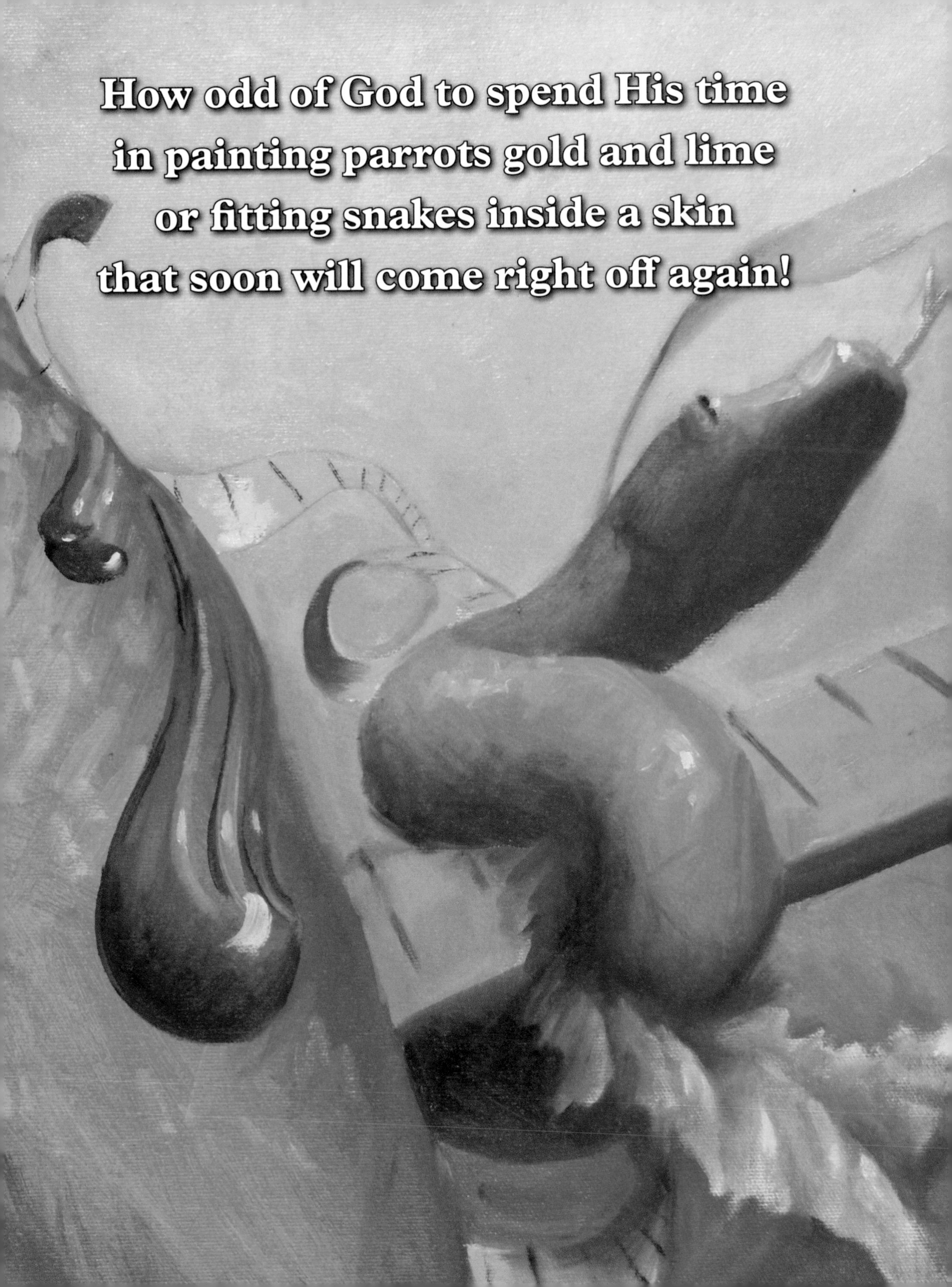

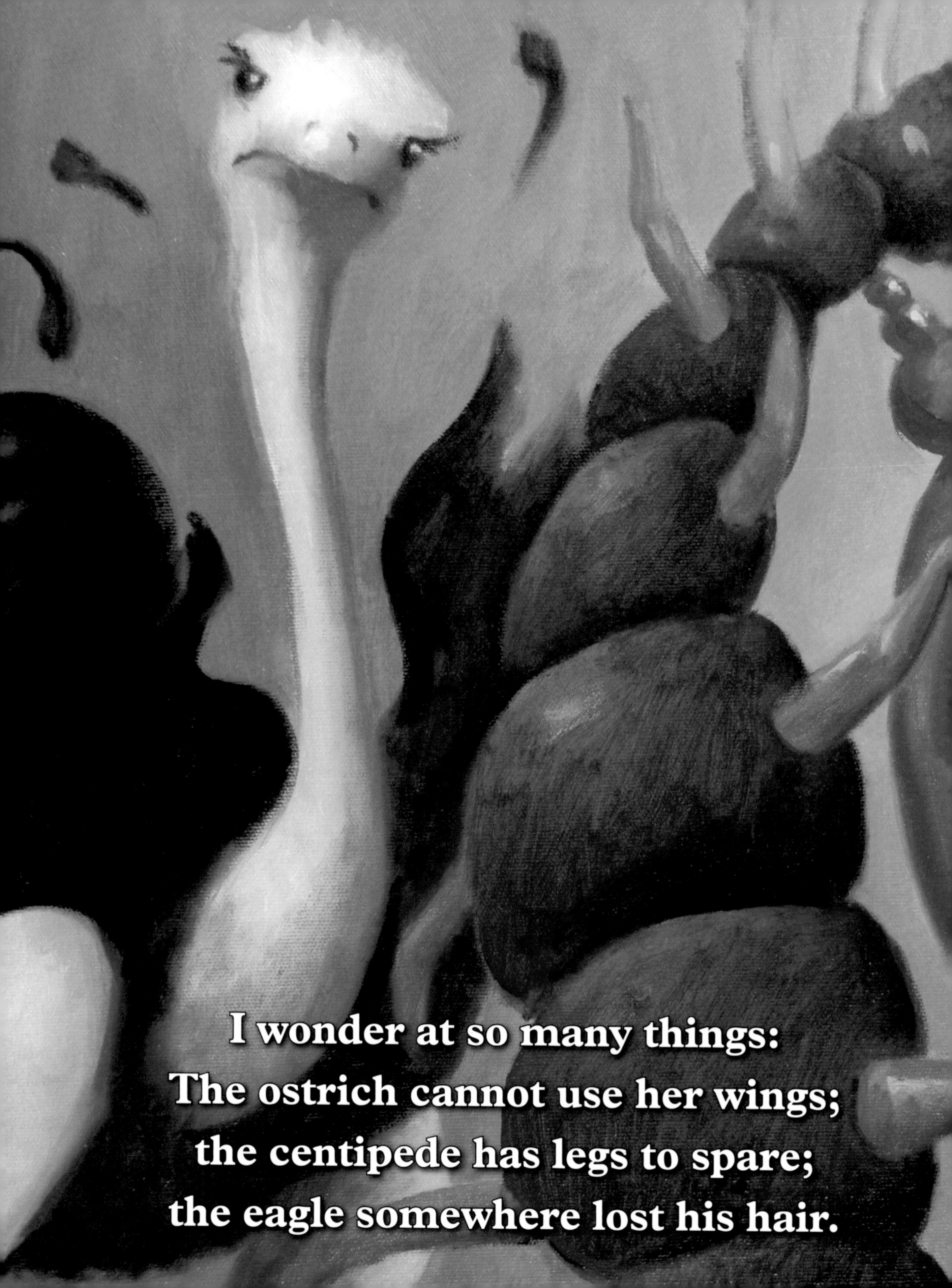

I wonder at so many things:
The ostrich cannot use her wings;
the centipede has legs to spare;
the eagle somewhere lost his hair.

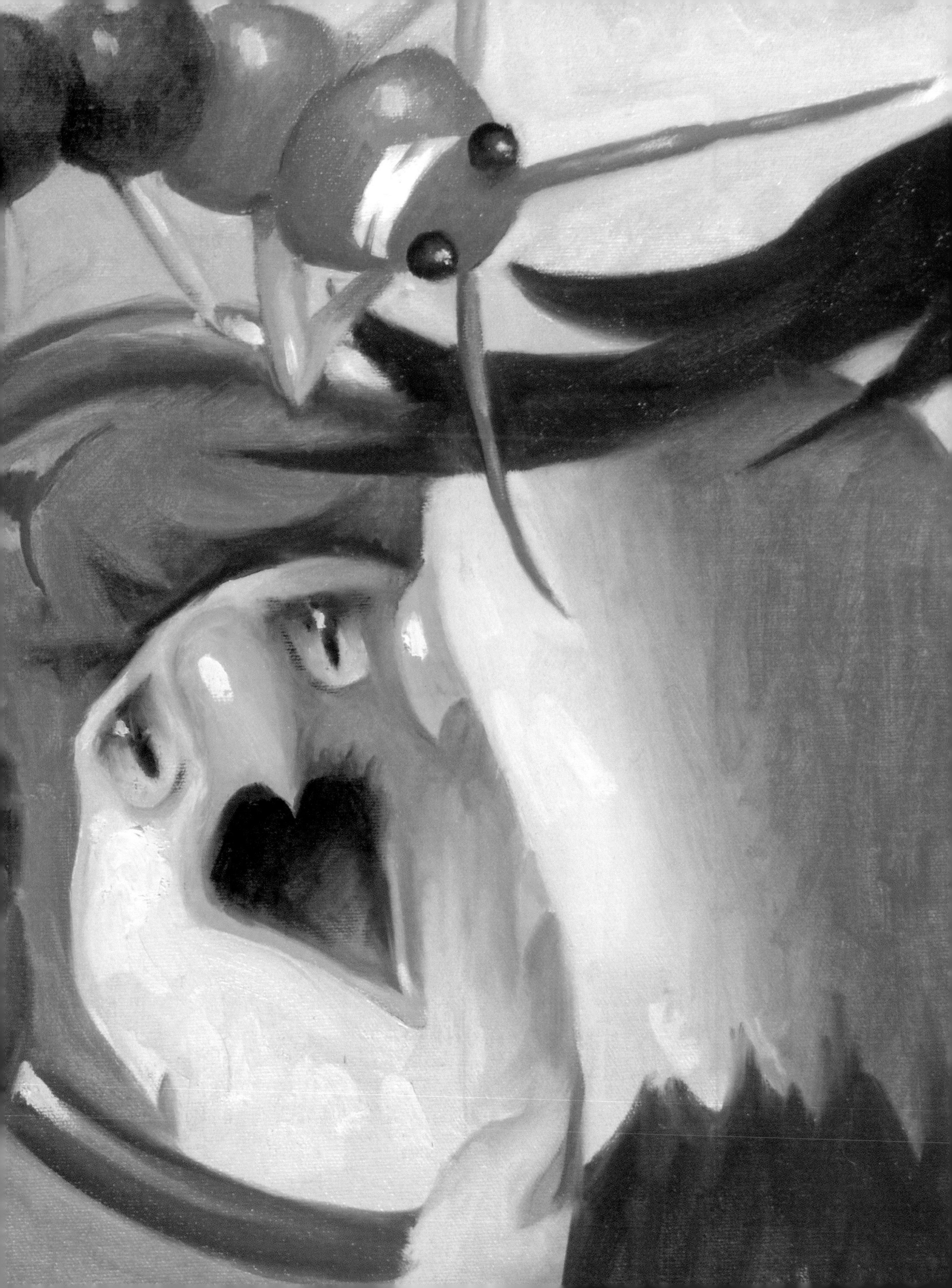

What's this? Who taught the seals to bark?
Did dogs give lessons on the Ark?
And why the fly? Who would complain
had Noah left it in the rain?

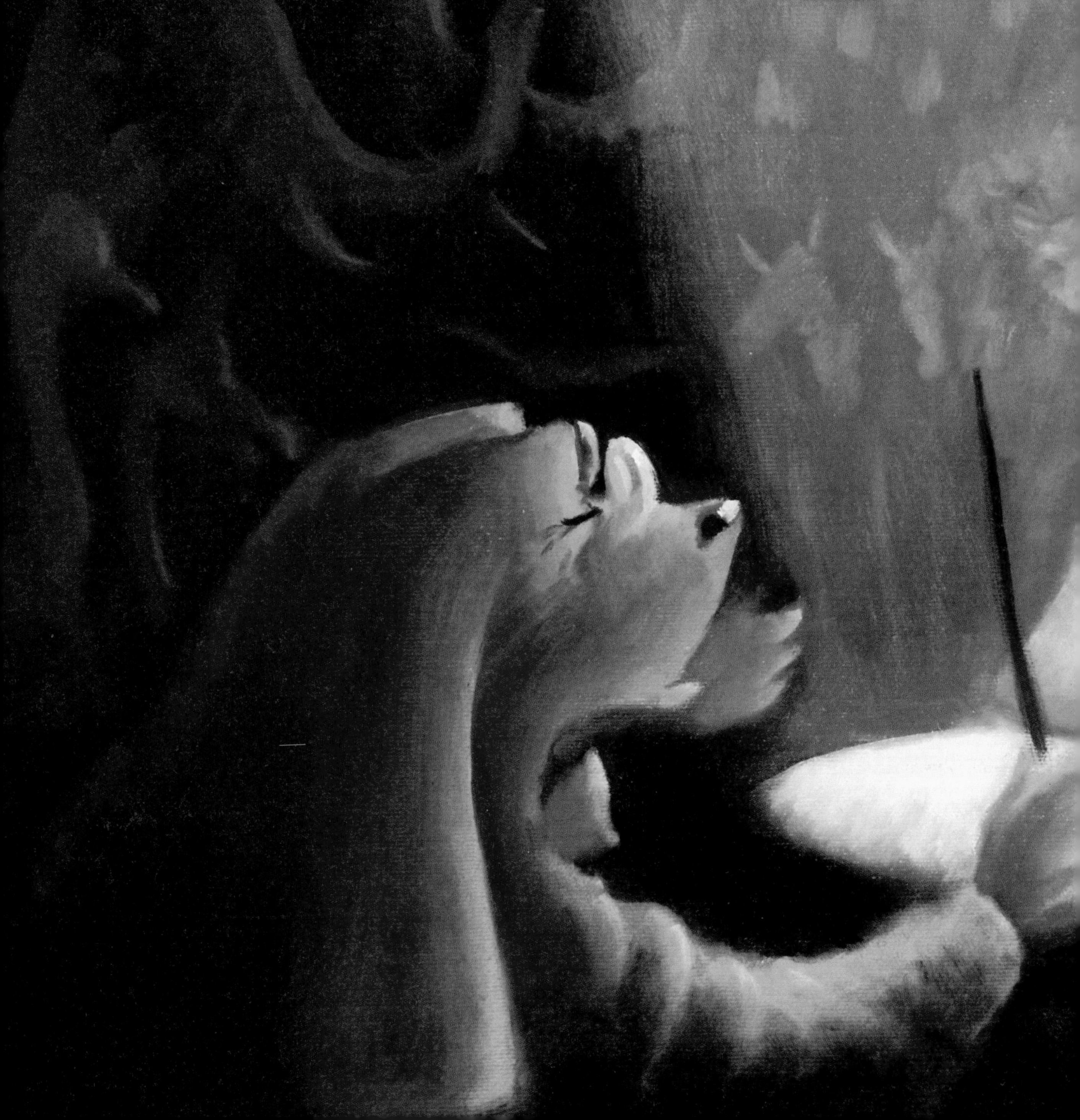

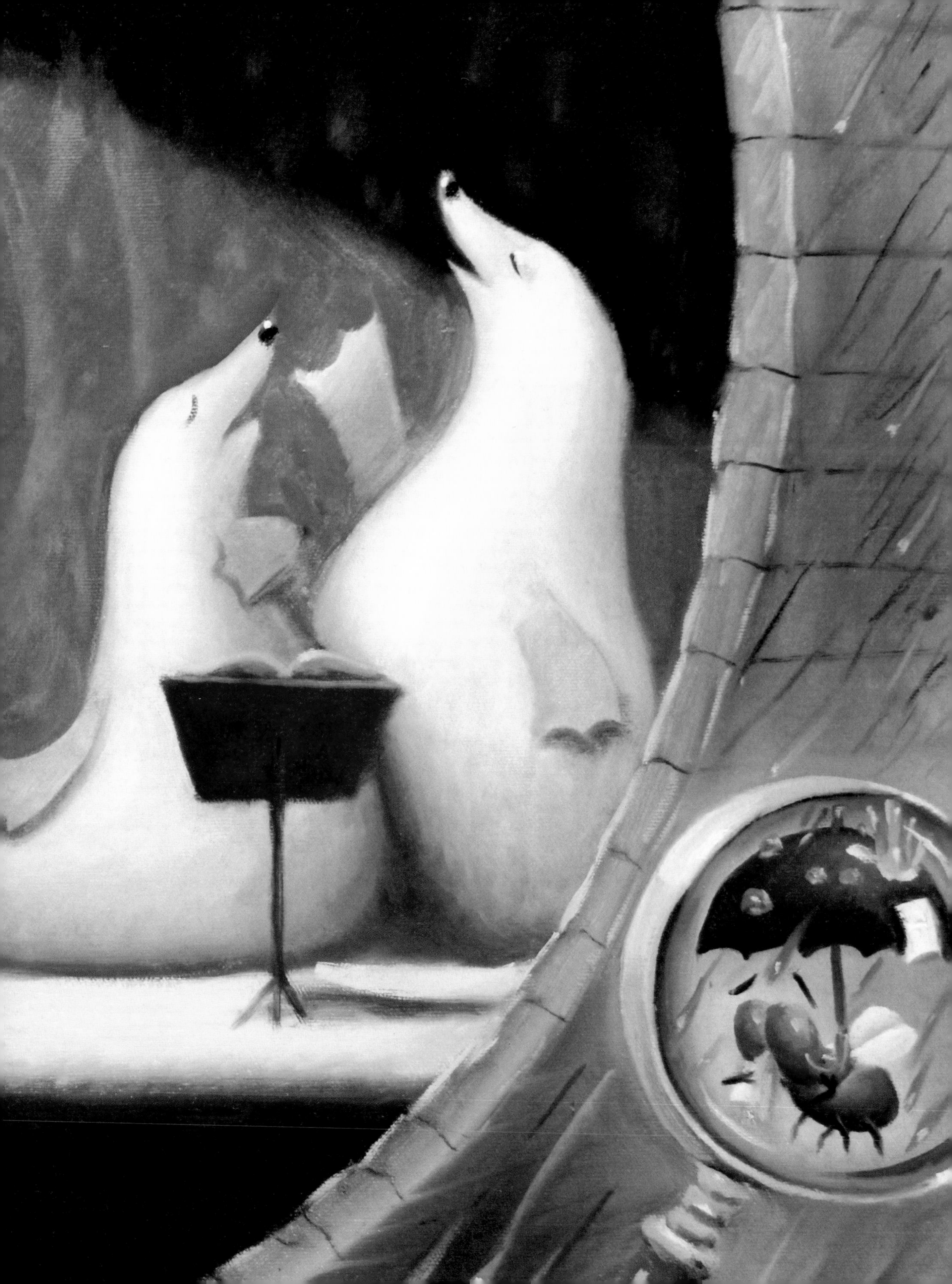

Yet of the creatures great and small,
God's wildest wonderment of all
has gathered all these in one place,

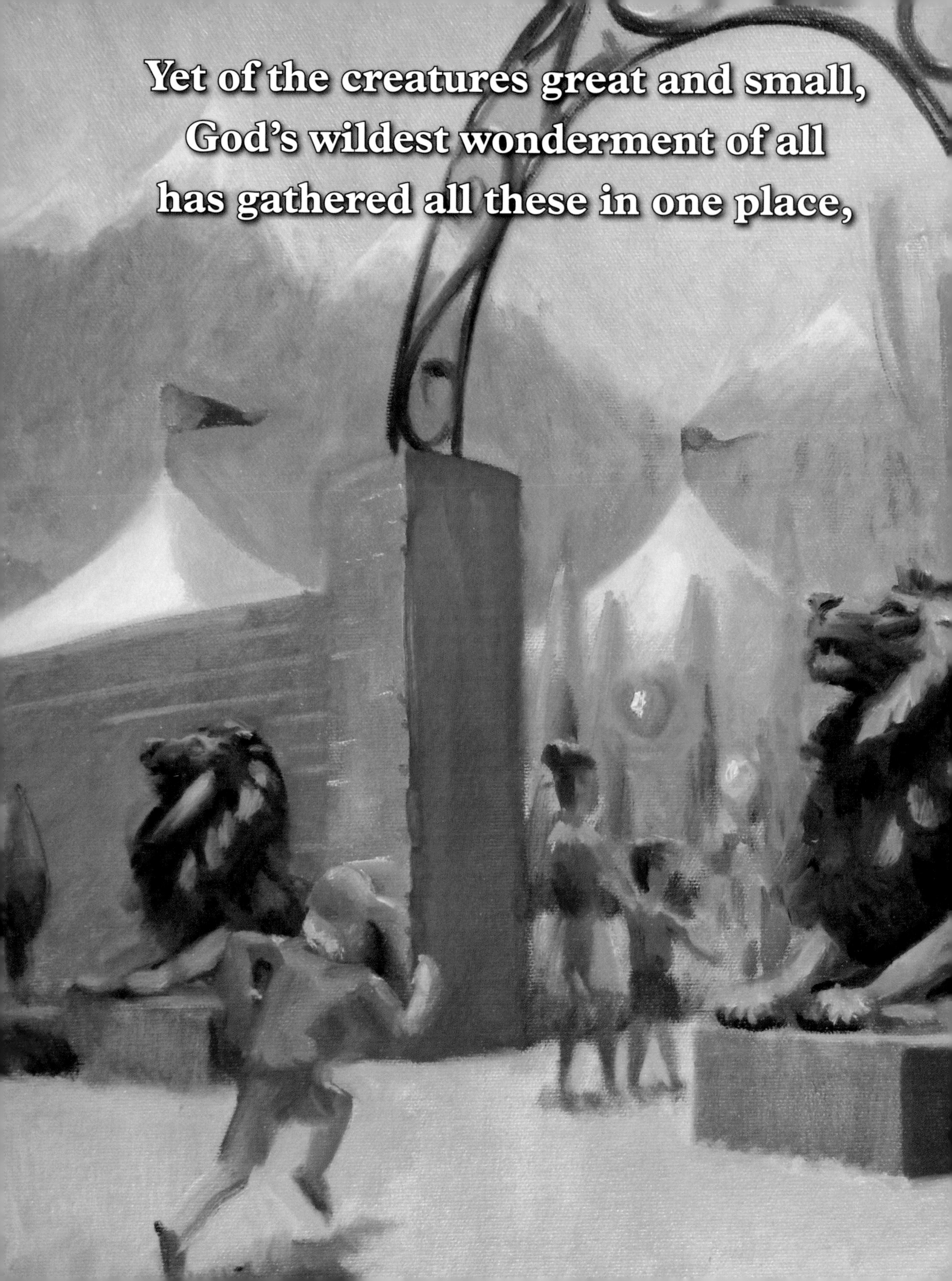

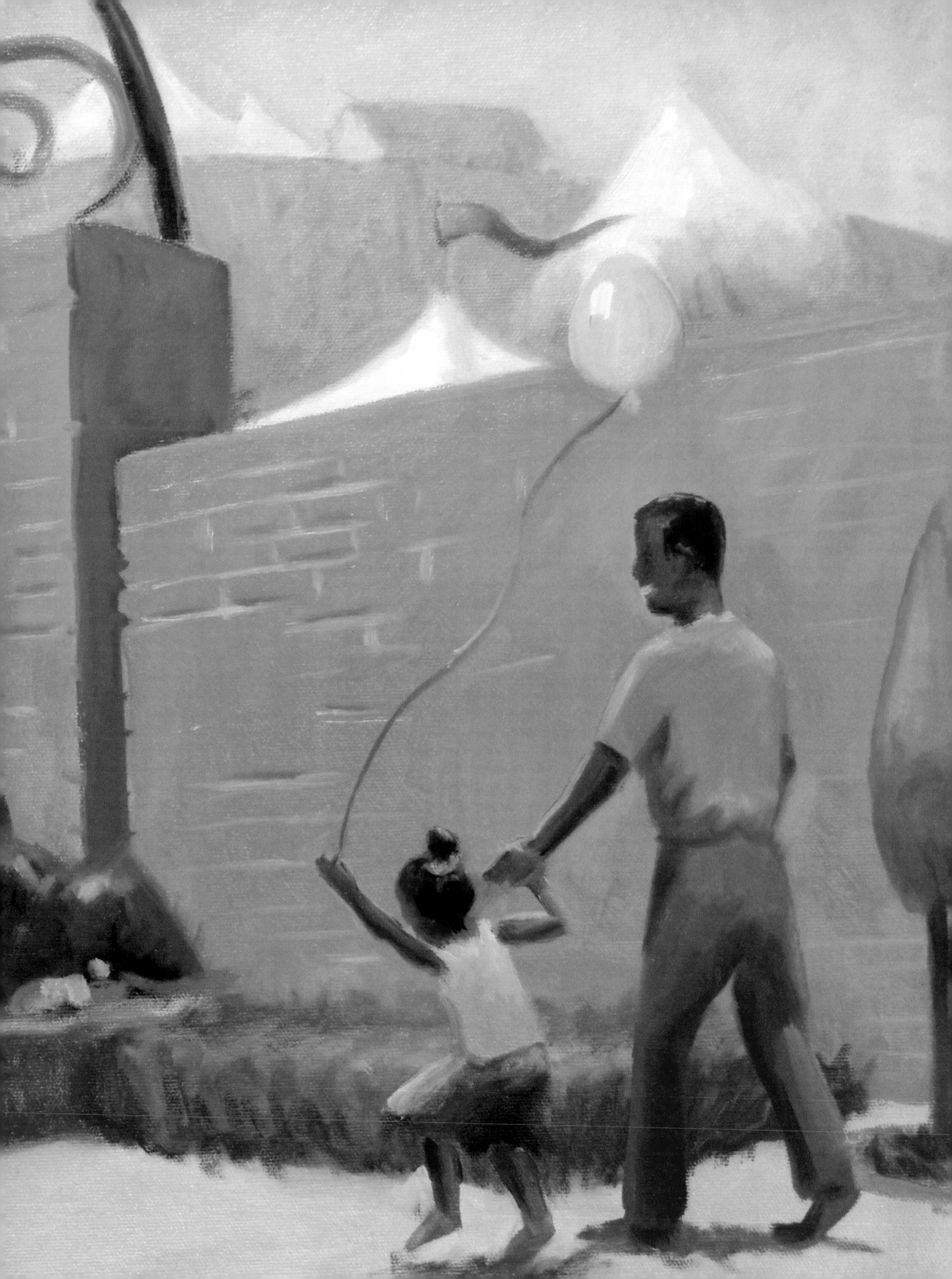

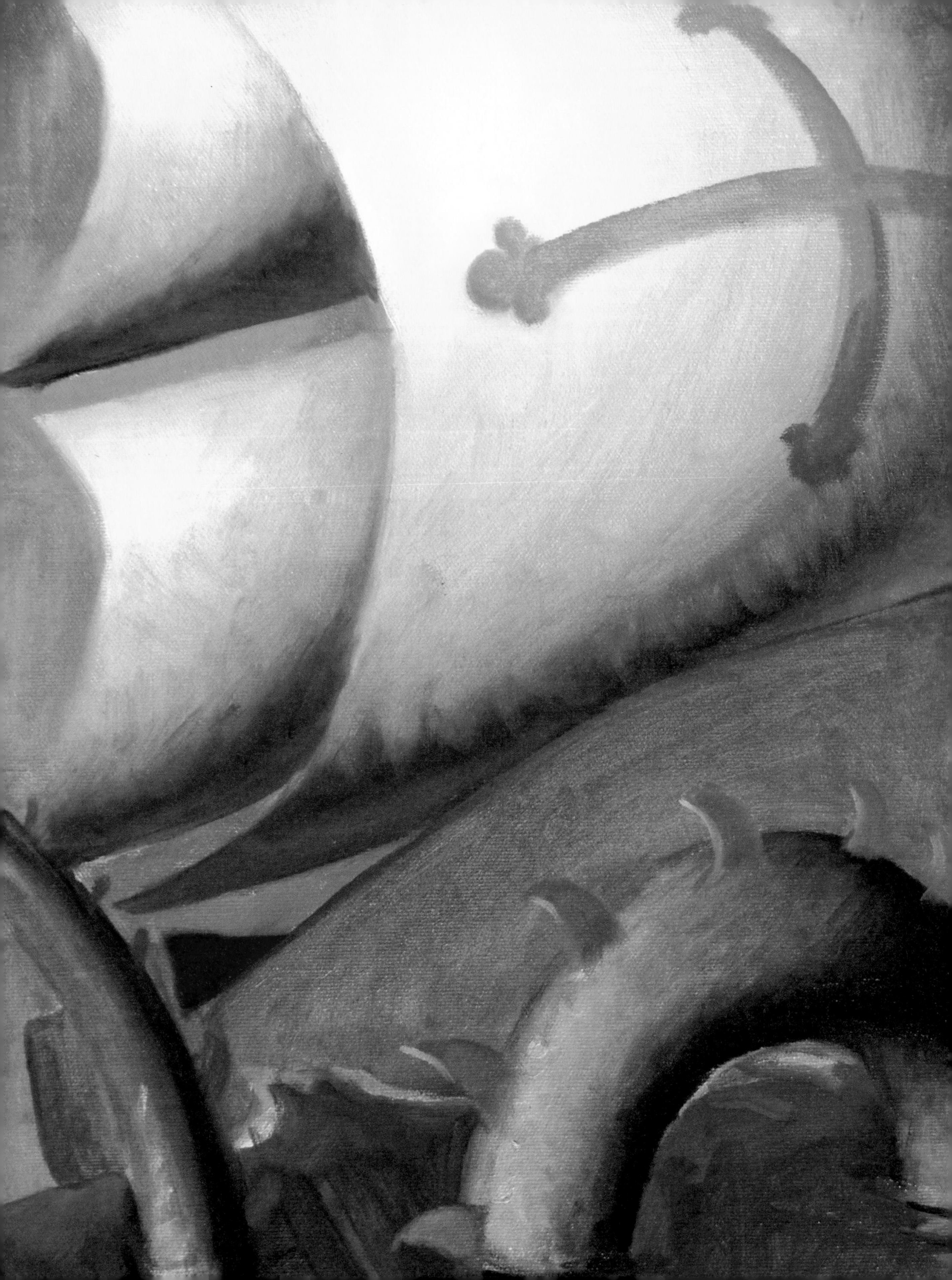

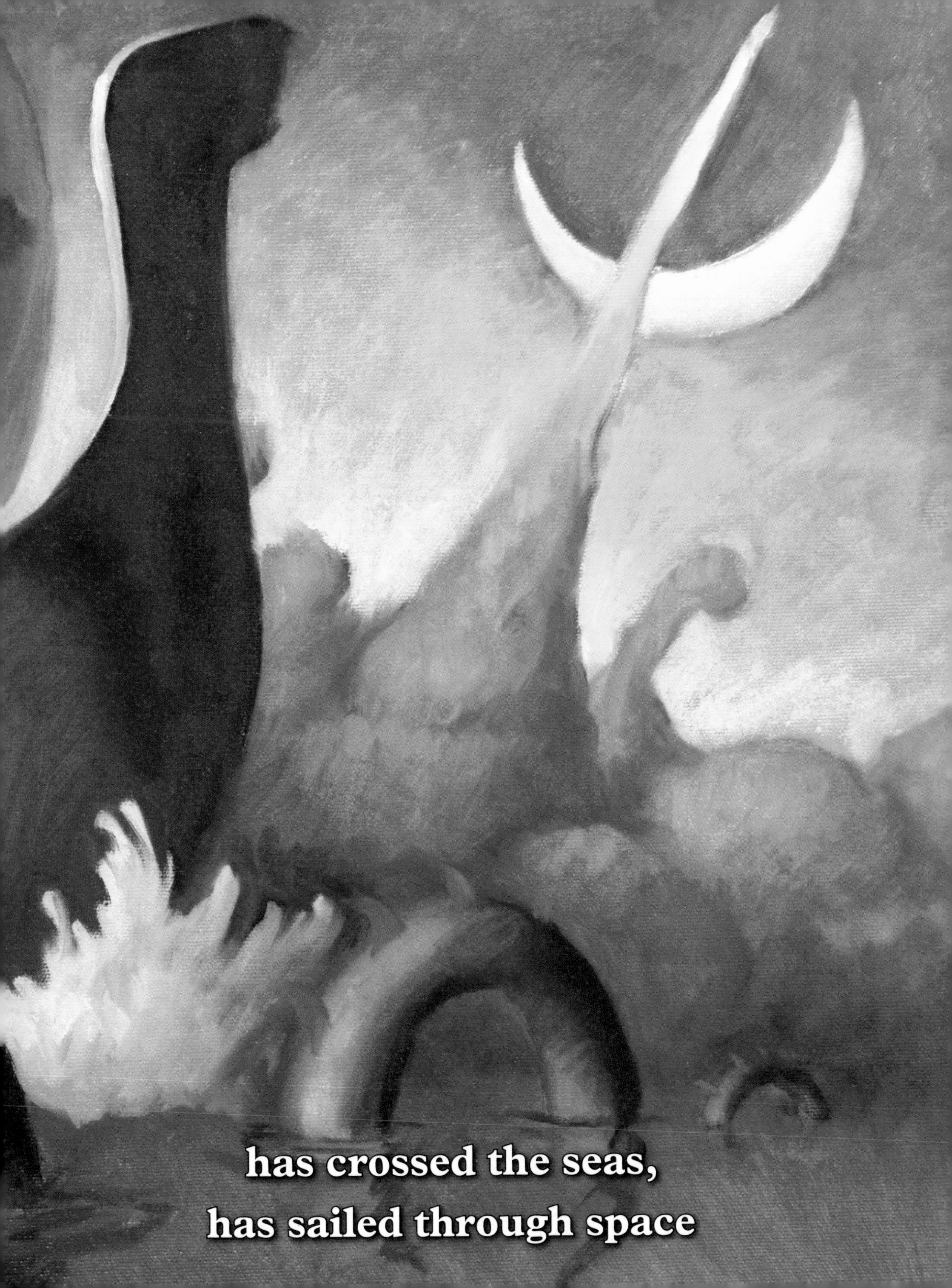

has crossed the seas,
has sailed through space

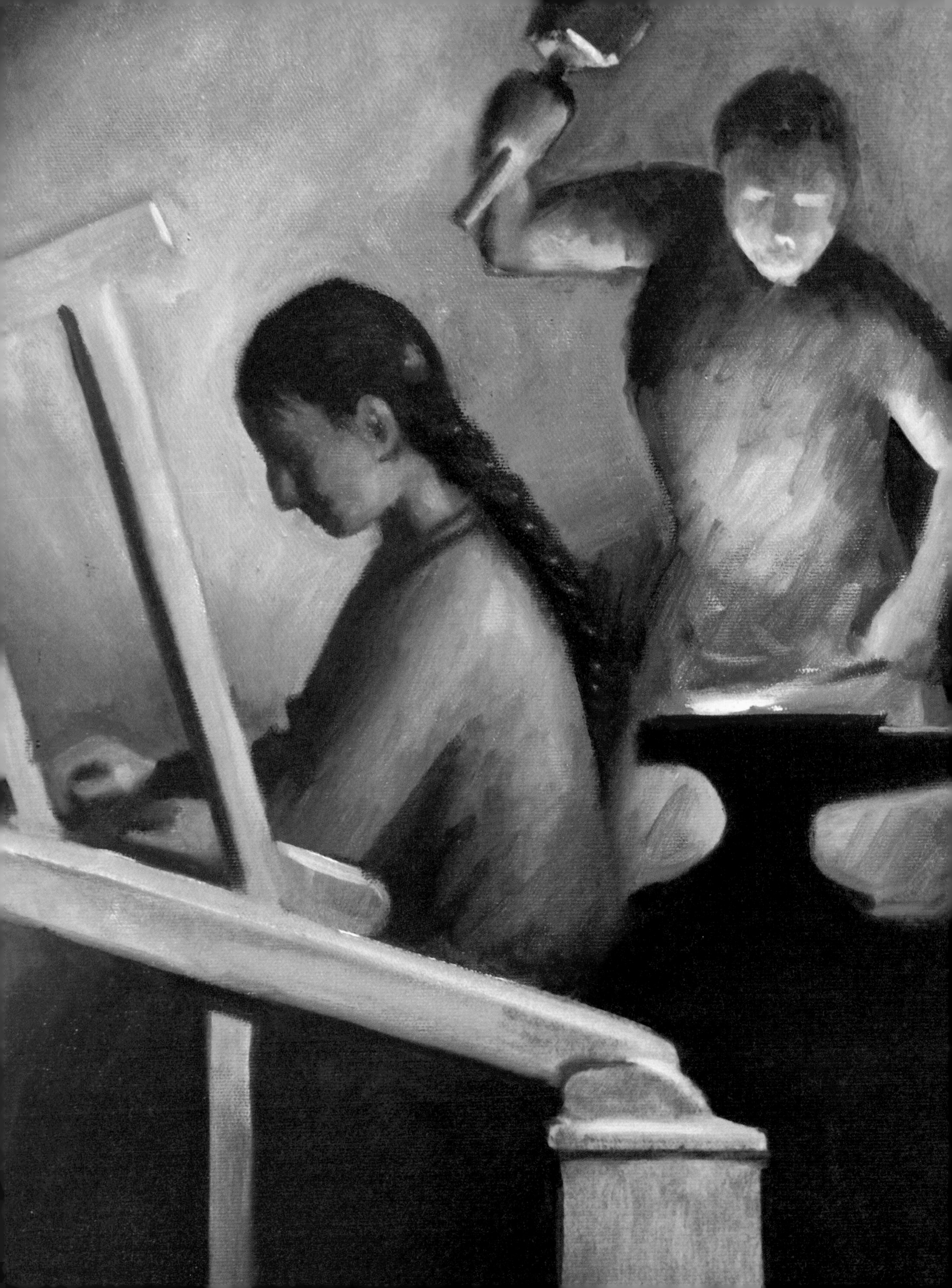

It has no fur; it weaves its own.
It tames the fire and carves the stone.

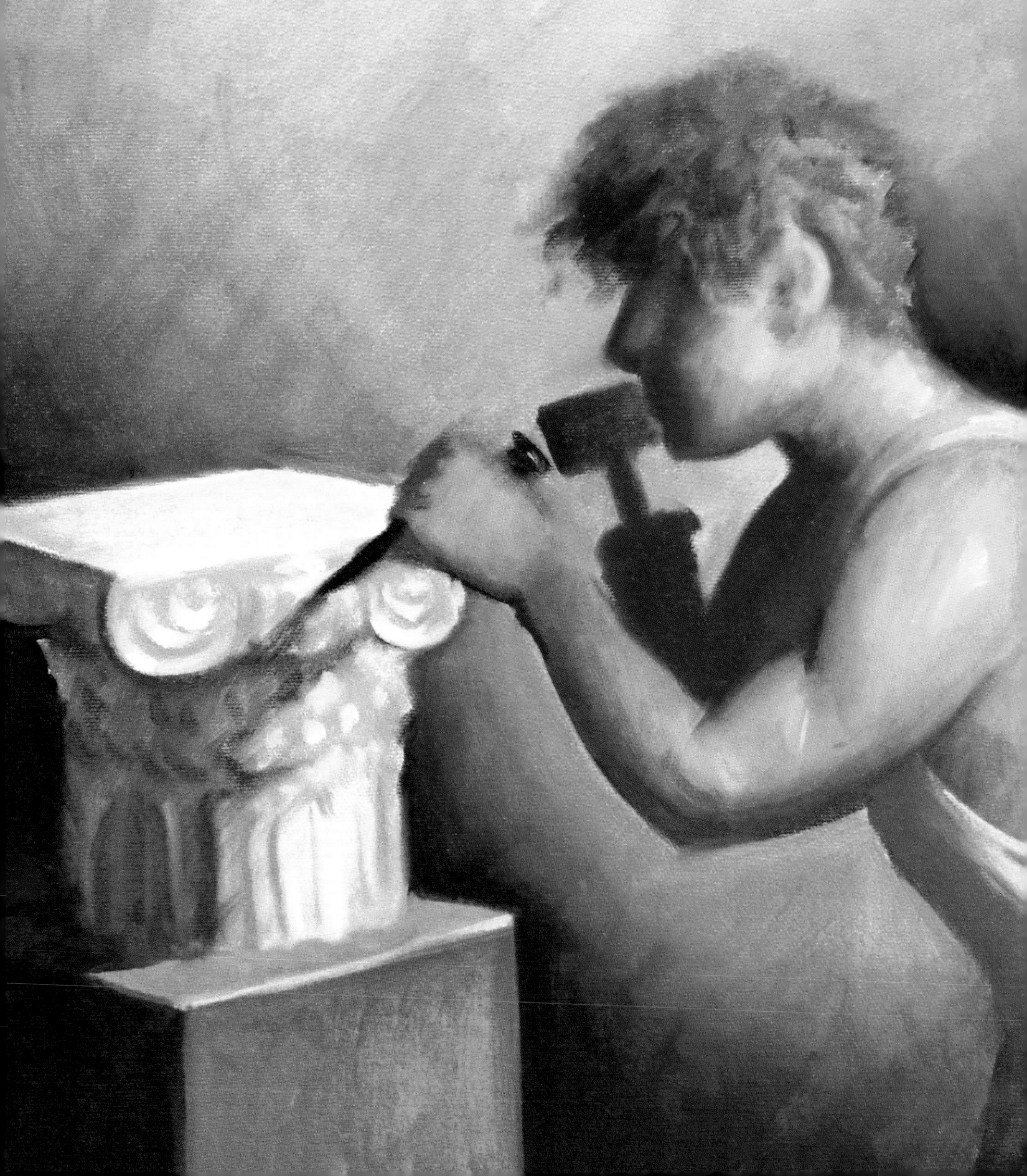

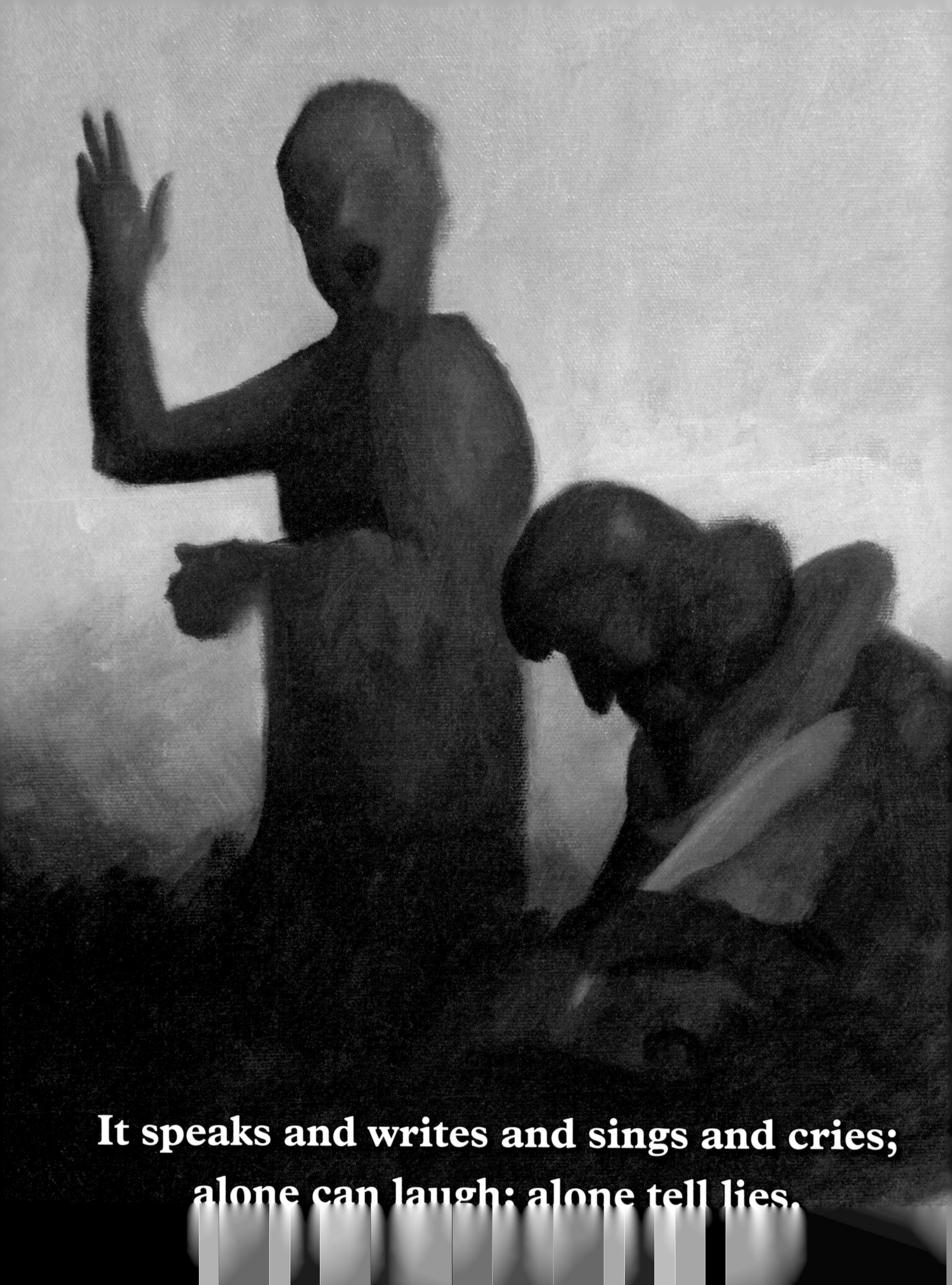

It speaks and writes and sings and cries;
alone can laugh; alone tell lies.

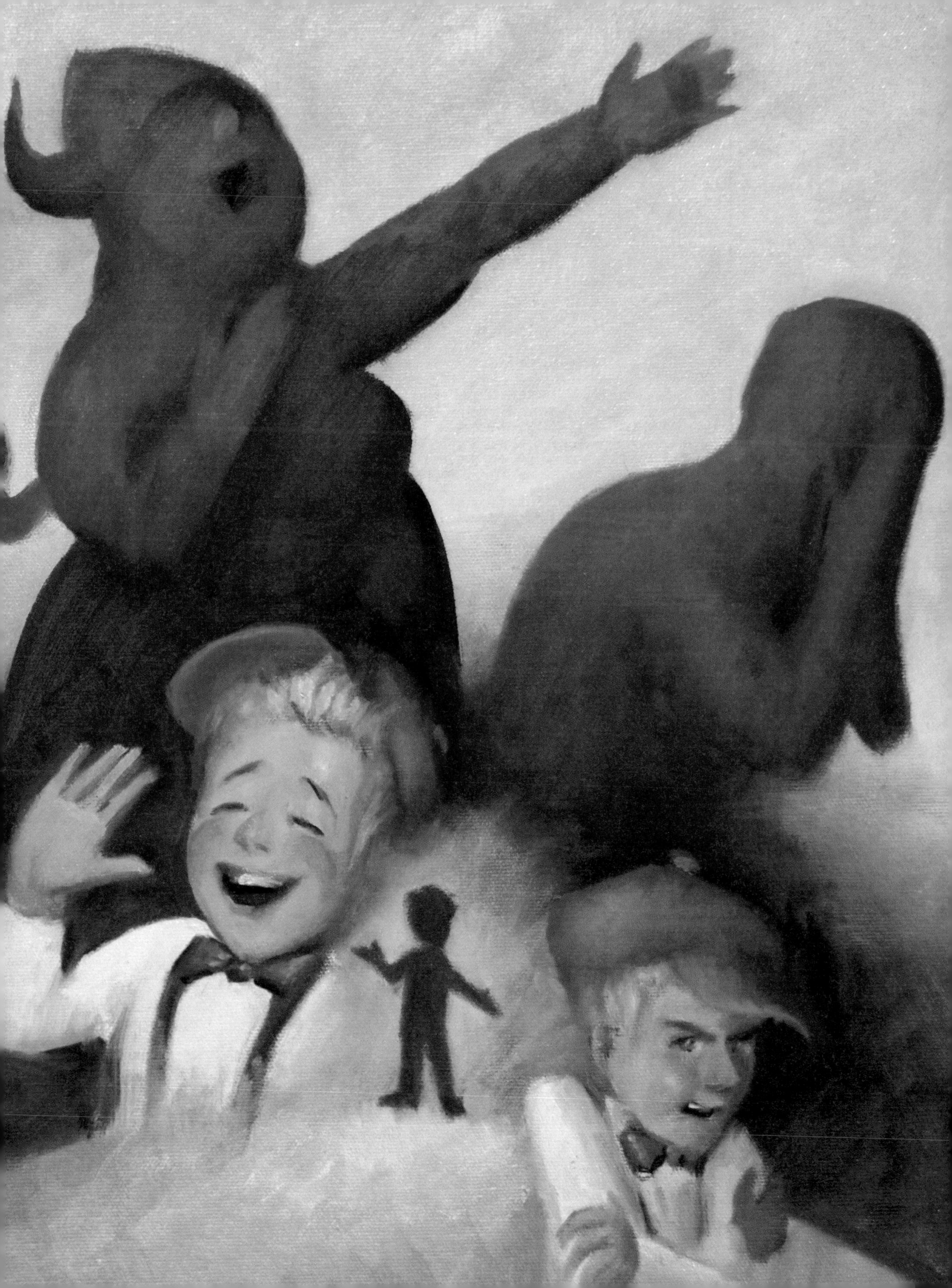

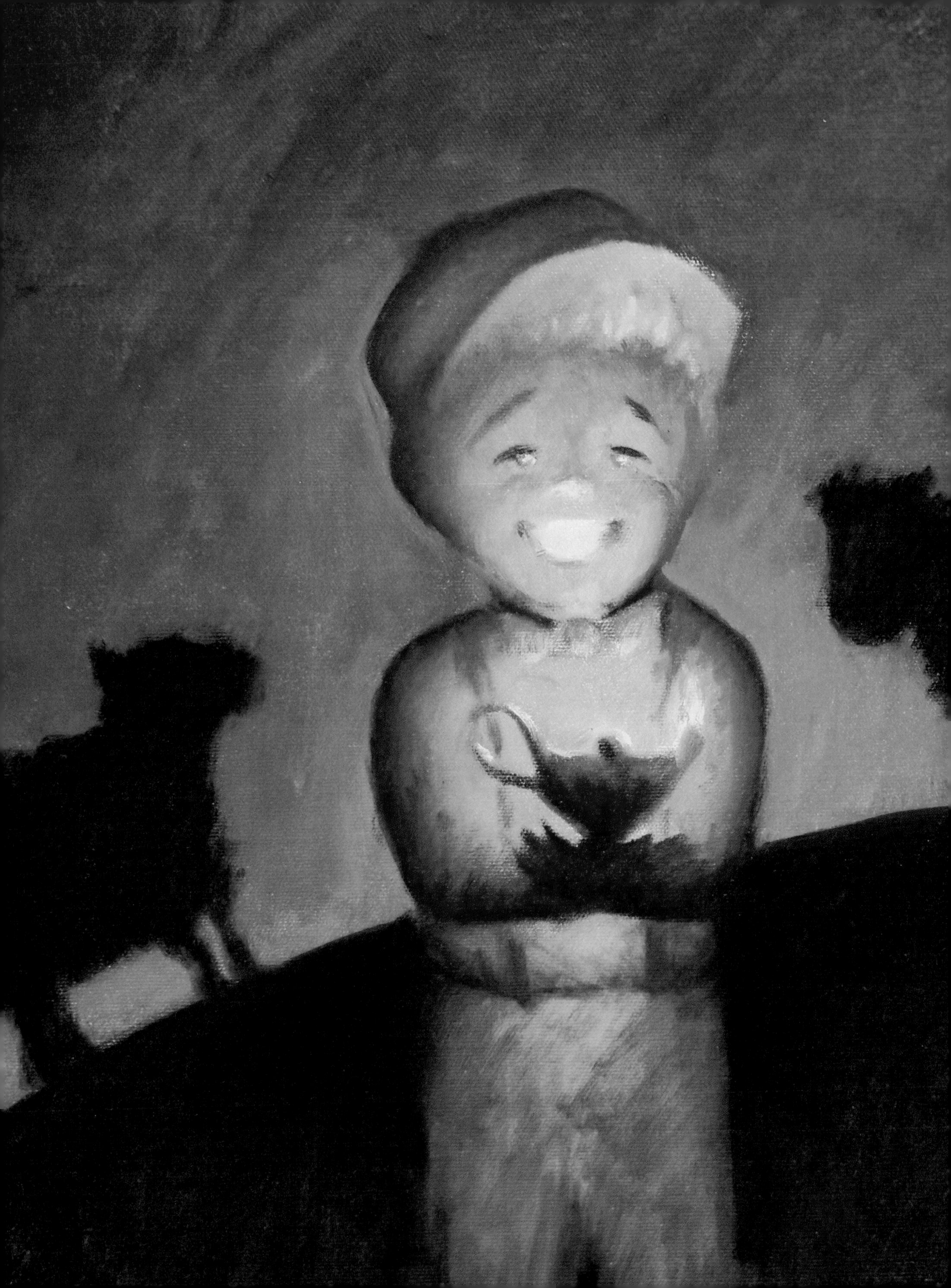

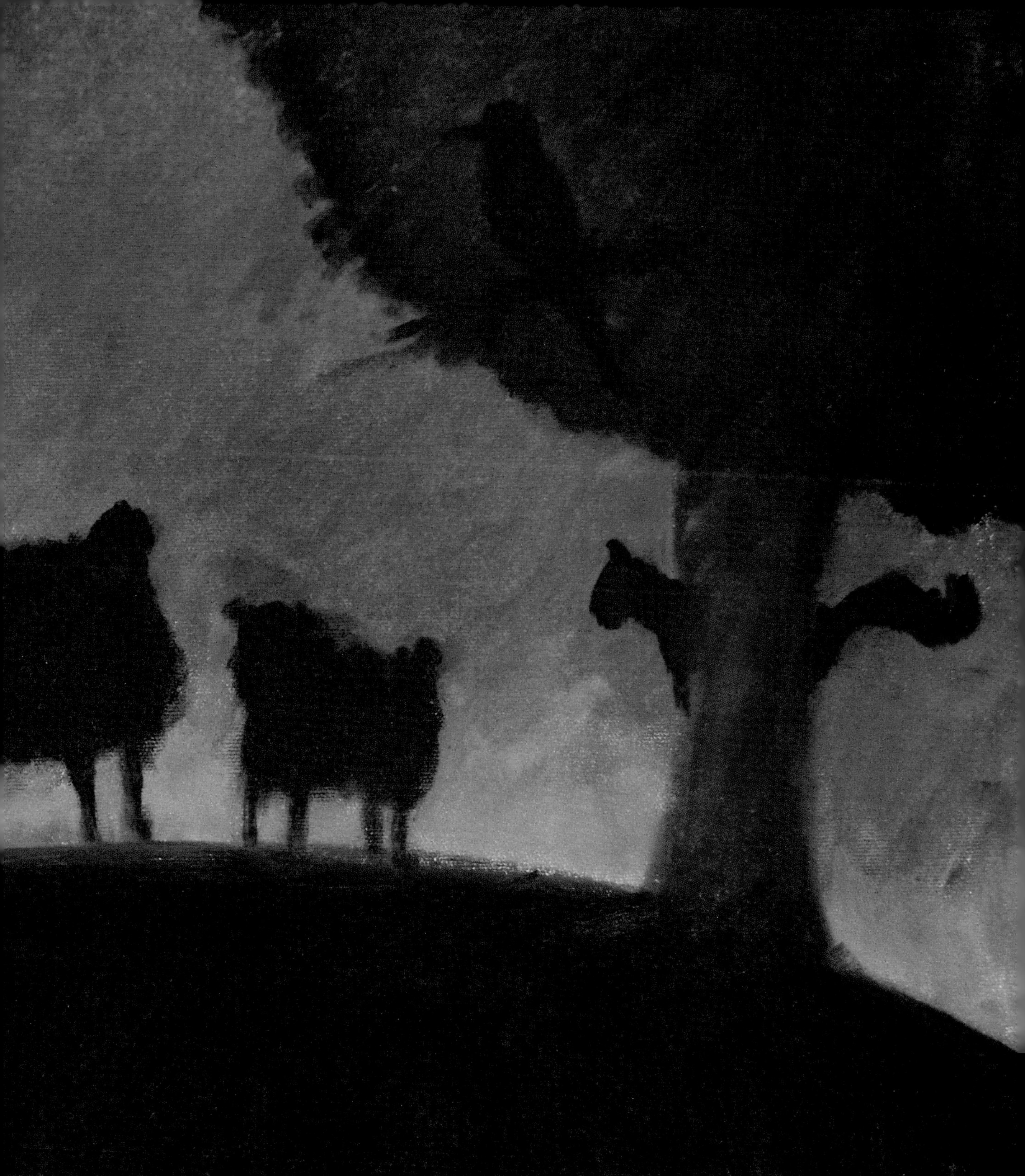

No animal of field or tree
can match the marvel I call ME!

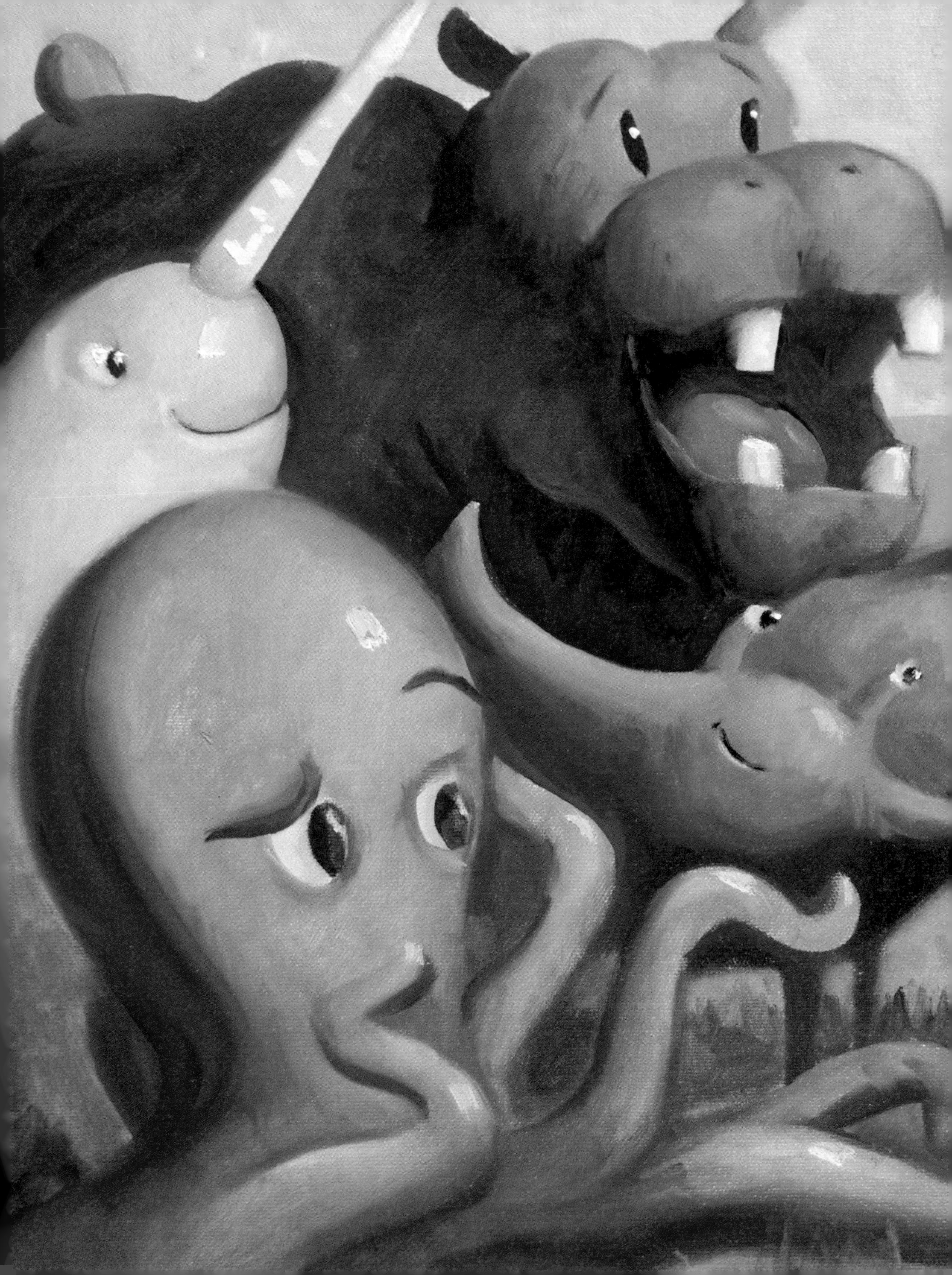

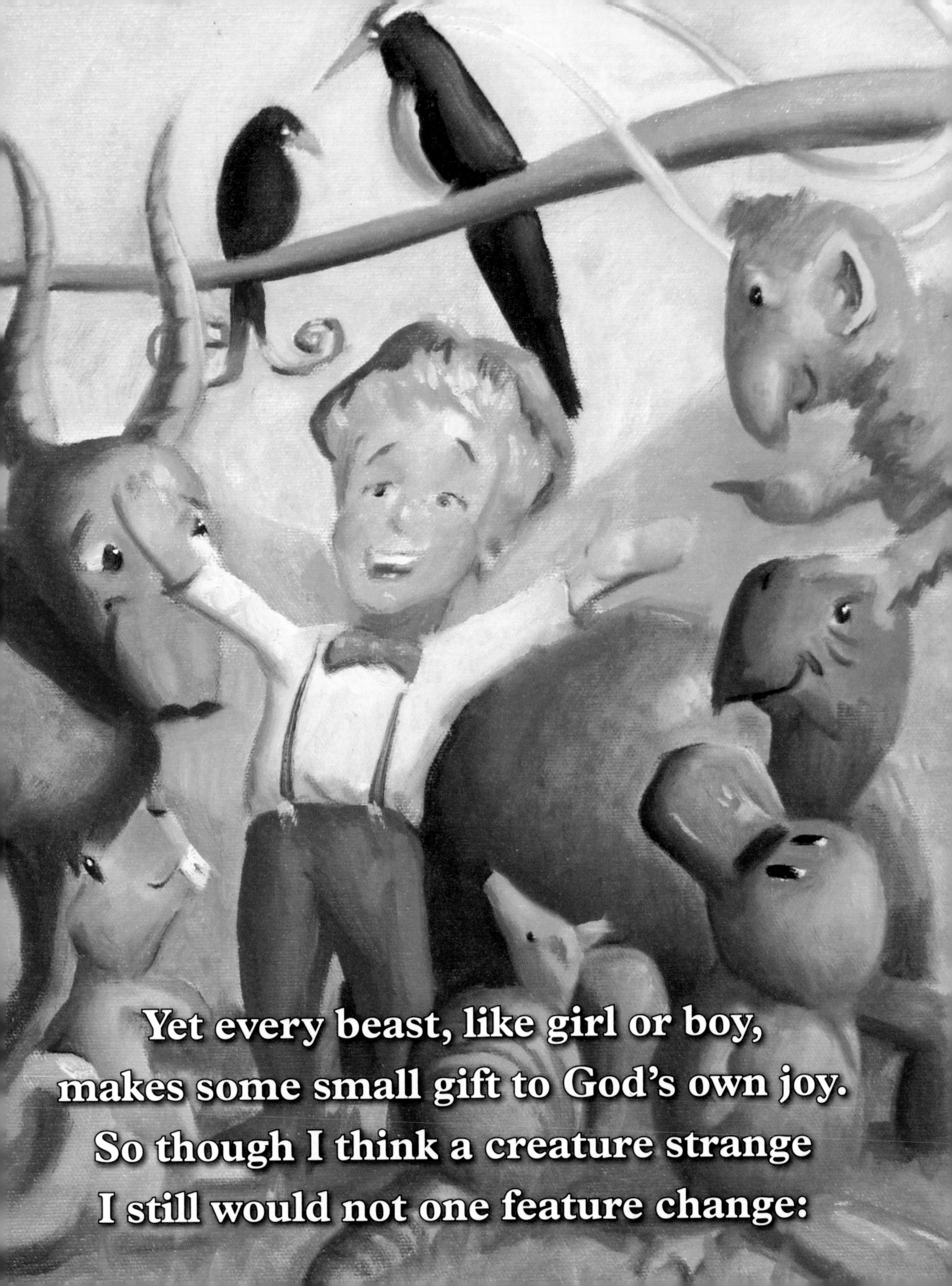

Yet every beast, like girl or boy,
makes some small gift to God's own joy.
So though I think a creature strange
I still would not one feature change:

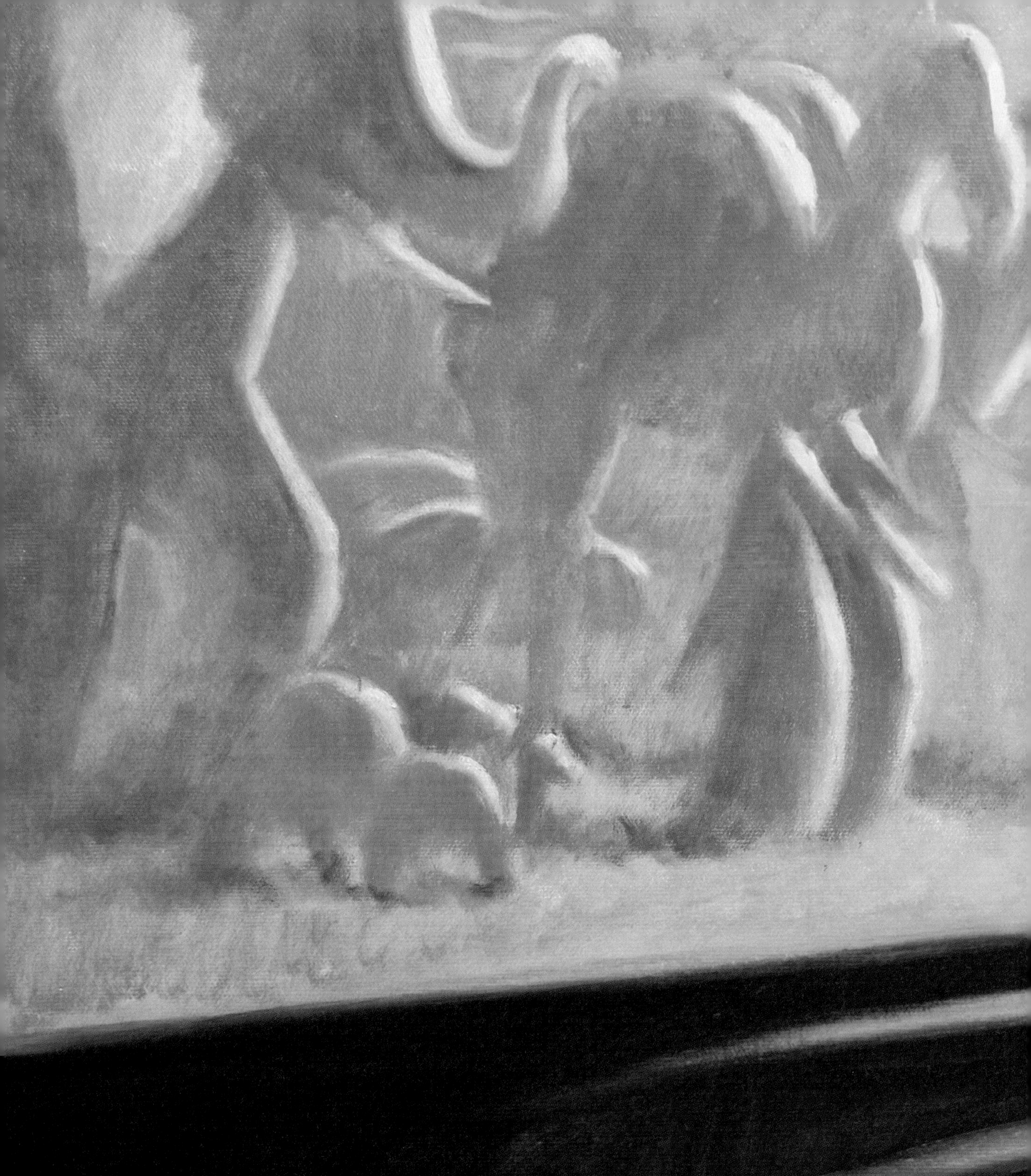

Each plays its part in Heaven's plan
and joins in Earth's great caravan.

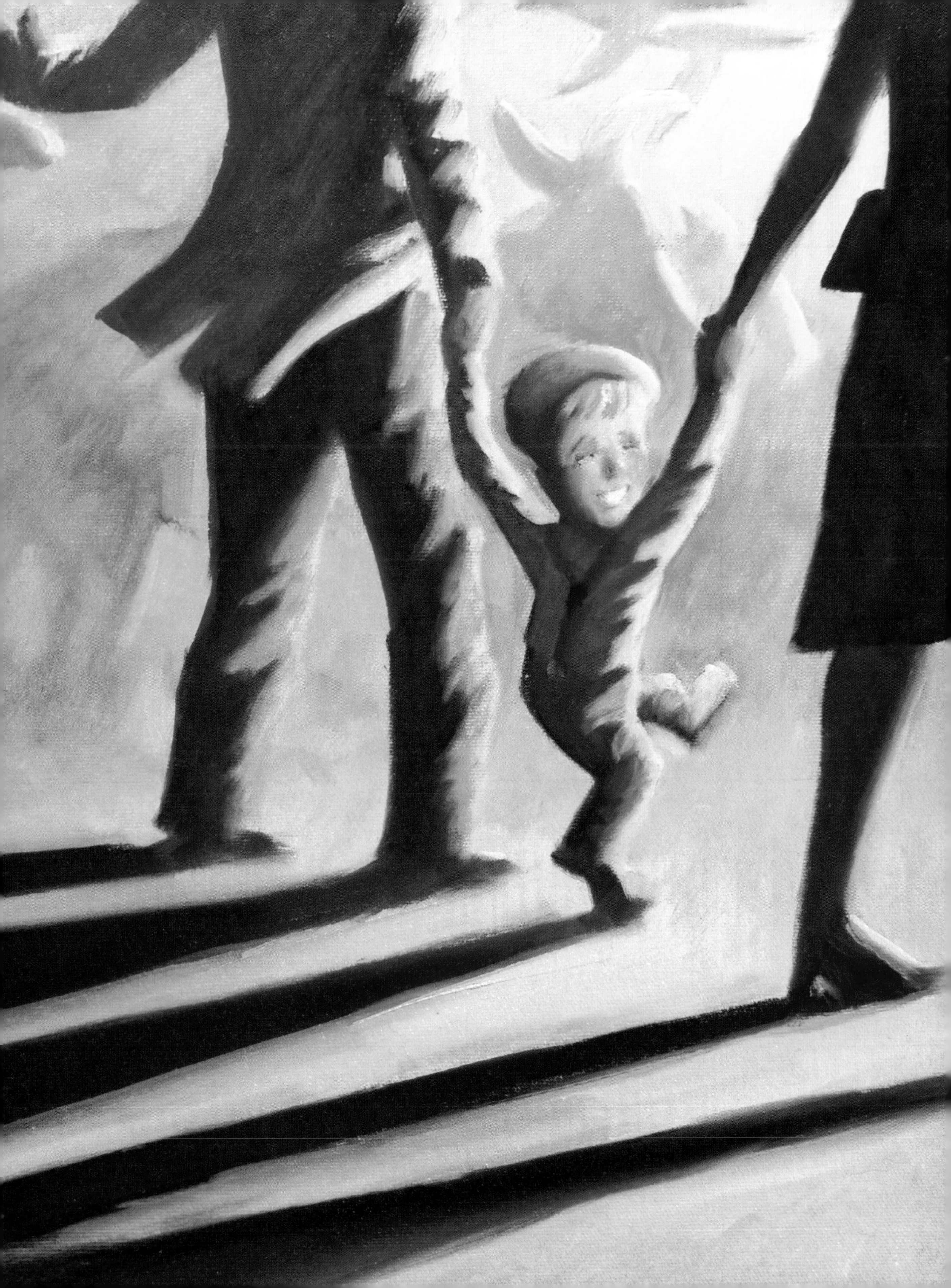

PAUL THIGPEN, PhD, is an award-winning journalist and the bestselling author of fifty-two books. Among his most popular works are *Manual for Spiritual Warfare* and *A Year With the Saints: Daily Meditations with the Holy Ones of God.* A convert to the Catholic faith, Paul has served the Church as a theology professor, historian, speaker, apologist, catechist, and member of the National Advisory Council of the United States Conference of Catholic Bishops. His work has been circulated worldwide and translated into fourteen languages.

JOHN FOLLEY is an independent artist and illustrator trained in the Boston School Tradition. John formerly taught at the Heights School in Potomac, Maryland, as head of their Art Department and is a currently Visiting Fellow and Art

Guild Master at the Thomas More College of Liberal Arts in Merrimack, New Hampshire. John has done illustration work for books, magazines, and businesses and his figurative fine art work includes portraits, still life, illuminations, and landscape paintings in homes, businesses, and churches across the United States. His studio is on the historic town green in Lancaster, Massachusetts, where he also resides with his wife, Deirdre, and their four young children. John advocates for a revival of true standards for beauty in Art at www.johnfolley.com.